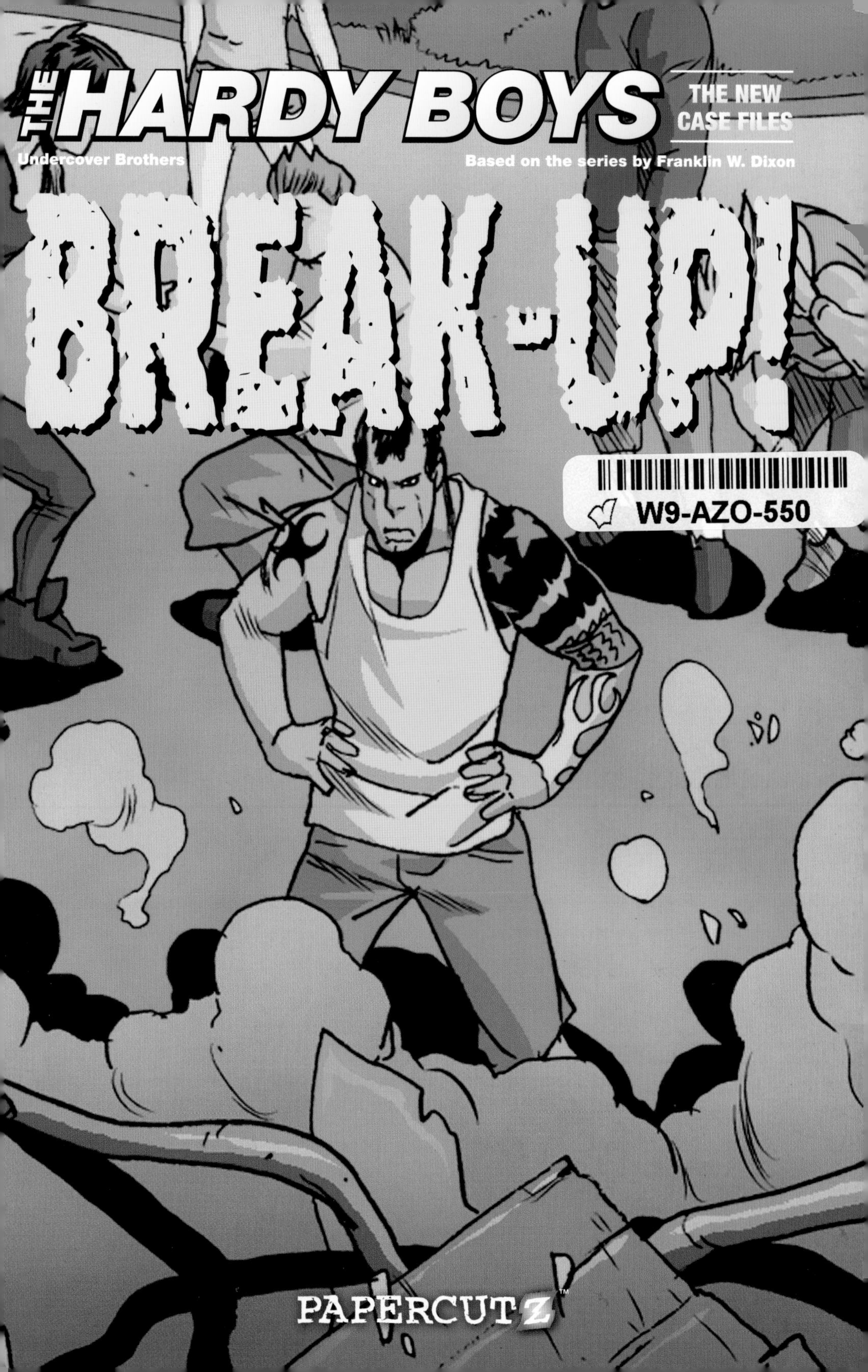
THE HARDY BOYS
THE NEW CASE FILES
Undercover Brothers
Based on the series by Franklin W. Dixon
BREAK-UP!
W9-AZO-550
PAPERCUTZ

THE HARDY BOYS GRAPHIC NOVELS FROM PAPERCUTZ

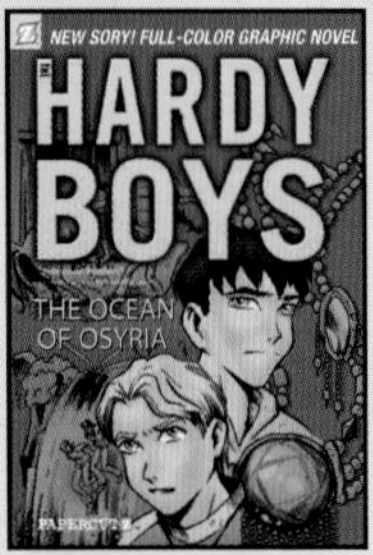

#1"The Ocean of Osyria"

#2 "Identity Theft"

#3 "Mad House"

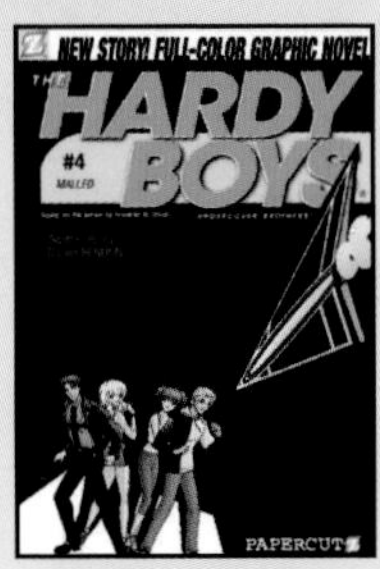

#4 "Malled"

#5 "Sea You, Sea Me!"

#6 "Hyde & Shriek"

#7 "The Opposite Numbers"

#8 "Board To Death"

#9 "To Die Or Not To Die?"

#10 "A Hardy Day's Night"

#11 "Abracadeath"

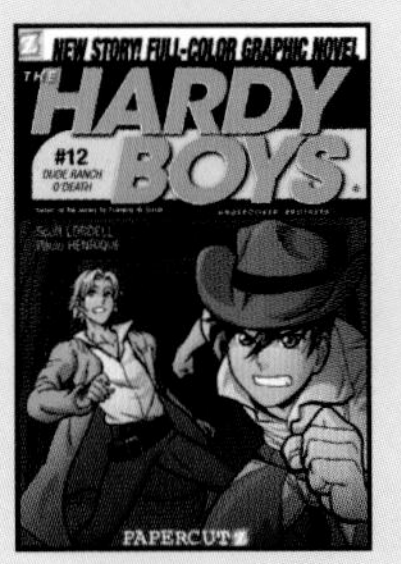

#12 "Dude Ranch O' Death!"

#13 "The Deadliest Stunt"

#14 "Haley Danielle's Top Eight!"

#15 "Live Free, Die Hardy!"

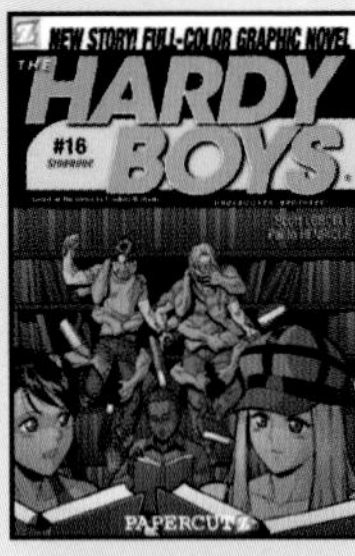

#16 "Shhhhhh!"

#17 "Word Up!"

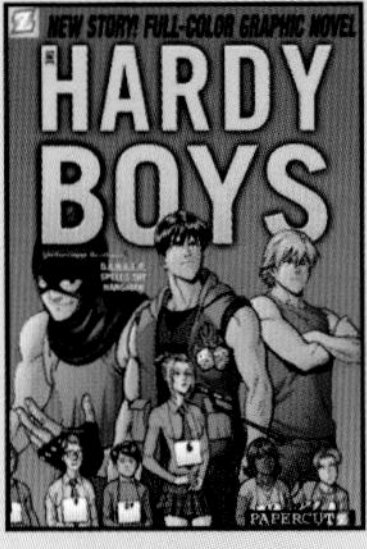

#18 "D.A.N.G.E.R Spells the Hangman"

#19 "Chaos at 30,000 Feet"

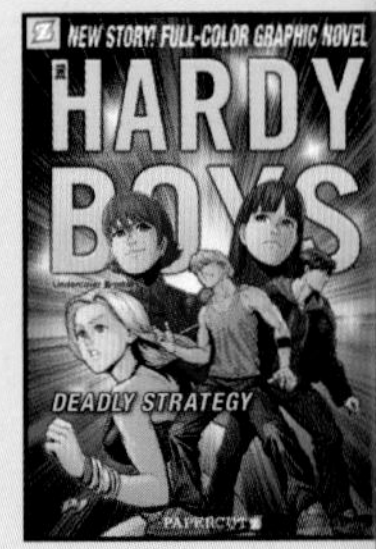

#20 "Deadly Strategy"

$7.95 each in paperback, $12.95 each in hardcover except #20, $8.99pb/$13.99hc.
Available through all booksellers.

See more at www.papercutz.com

Or you can order through us: please add $4.00 for postage and handling for the first book, and add $1.00 for each additional book. Please make check payable to NBM Publishing. Send to: Papercutz, 1200 County Rd., Rte 523, Flemin ton, NJ 08222 or call 800 886 1223 (9-6 EST M-F) MC-Visa-Amex accepted

Undercover Brothers

BREAK-UP!

GERRY CONWAY
Writer

PAULO HENRIQUE
Artist

Based on the series by FRANKLIN W. DIXON

New York

"Break-Up"
GERRY CONWAY - Writer
PAULO HENRIQUE - Artist
LAURIE E. SMITH - Colorist
BRYAN SENKA - Letterer
SHELLY STERNER & CHRIS NELSON - Production
MICHAEL PETRANEK - Associate Editor
JIM SALICRUP
Editor-in-Chief

ISBN: 978-1-59707-242-7 paperback edition
ISBN: 978-1-59707-243-4 hardcover edition

Printed in China
January 2011 by O.G. Printing Productions, LTD.
Unit 2 & 3, 5/F Lemmi Centre
50 Hoi Yen Road
Kwon Tong, Kowloon

Distributed by Macmillan.
First Printing

CHAPTER ONE:
ANOTHER FINE MESS
YOU REALIZE, DON'T YOU,
THIS IS TOTALLY YOUR FAULT.
MY FAULT?
IF WE'D HANDLED THIS THE WAY I WANTED, WE'D BE REPORTING IN TO A.T.A.C.* HOW WE'D SOLVED ANOTHER CASE RIGHT ABOUT NOW.
BUT NO --
*AMERICAN TEENS AGAINST CRIME
REALLY, JOE?
YOU REALLY THINK THIS IS THE TIME TO DEBATE DIFFERENT METHODS OF INVESTIGATING CRIMES?
WHY NOT, FRANK?

ULTIMATE
FLAMES

IT'S NOT LIKE WE'RE *GOING* ANYWHERE.

CLICK
RATTTTTLE-KLINK KLINK KLINK
KLANK
KLANK
KLANK
WHOA, WHOA!
WHOA, WHOA, WHOA!!
CLICK
KLACK
OOOF
UMMMF

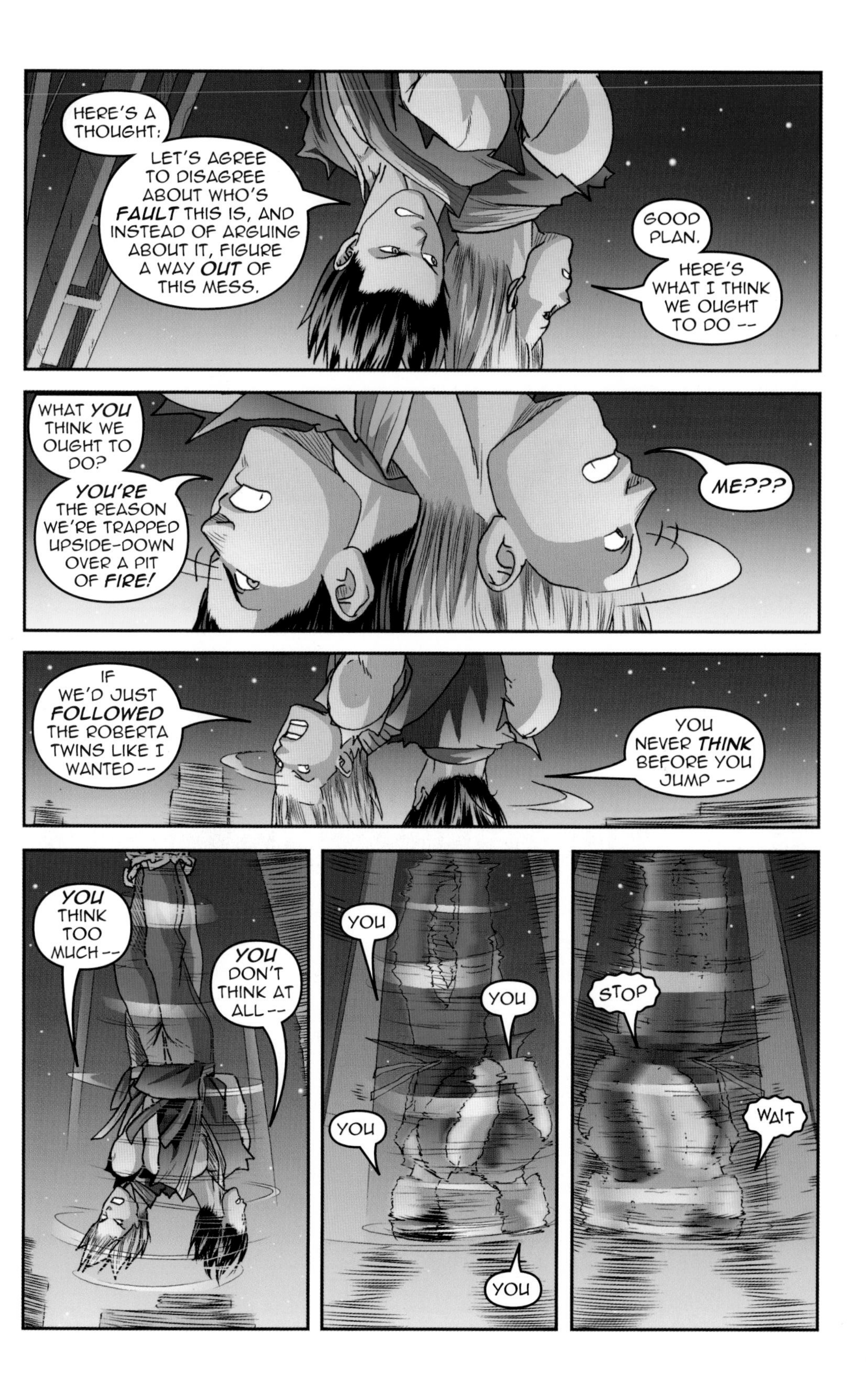
HERE'S A THOUGHT:
LET'S AGREE TO DISAGREE ABOUT WHO'S FAULT THIS IS, AND INSTEAD OF ARGUING ABOUT IT, FIGURE A WAY OUT OF THIS MESS.
GOOD PLAN.
HERE'S WHAT I THINK WE OUGHT TO DO --
WHAT YOU THINK WE OUGHT TO DO?
YOU'RE THE REASON WE'RE TRAPPED UPSIDE-DOWN OVER A PIT OF FIRE!
ME???
IF WE'D JUST FOLLOWED THE ROBERTA TWINS LIKE I WANTED --
YOU NEVER THINK BEFORE YOU JUMP --
YOU THINK TOO MUCH --
YOU DON'T THINK AT ALL --
YOU
YOU
YOU
YOU
STOP
WAIT

UNG
UHRP
I FEEL SICK.
PLEASE LET'S NOT DO THAT AGAIN.
LET'S TAKE A MOMENT.
RELAX.
THEN WORK THIS OUT.
OKAY BY ME.
BUT THIS IS *STILL YOUR FAULT!*

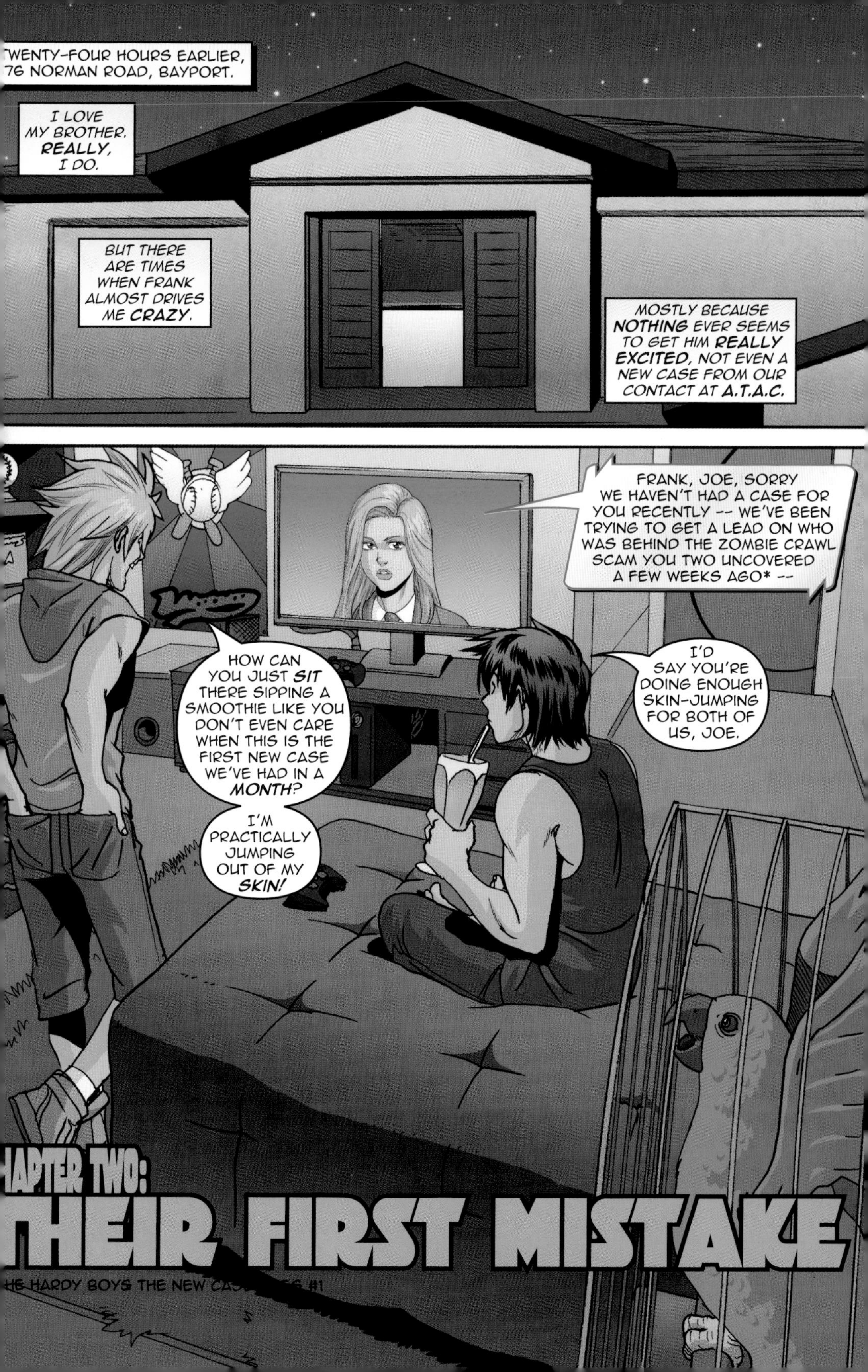

WENTY-FOUR HOURS EARLIER, 76 NORMAN ROAD, BAYPORT.
I LOVE MY BROTHER. **REALLY,** I DO.
BUT THERE ARE TIMES WHEN FRANK ALMOST DRIVES ME **CRAZY**.
MOSTLY BECAUSE **NOTHING** EVER SEEMS TO GET HIM **REALLY EXCITED**, NOT EVEN A NEW CASE FROM OUR CONTACT AT **A.T.A.C.**
FRANK, JOE, SORRY WE HAVEN'T HAD A CASE FOR YOU RECENTLY -- WE'VE BEEN TRYING TO GET A LEAD ON WHO WAS BEHIND THE ZOMBIE CRAWL SCAM YOU TWO UNCOVERED A FEW WEEKS AGO* --
HOW CAN YOU JUST ***SIT*** THERE SIPPING A SMOOTHIE LIKE YOU DON'T EVEN CARE WHEN THIS IS THE FIRST NEW CASE WE'VE HAD IN A ***MONTH***?
I'M PRACTICALLY JUMPING OUT OF MY ***SKIN!***
I'D SAY YOU'RE DOING ENOUGH SKIN-JUMPING FOR BOTH OF US, JOE.
HAPTER TWO:
HEIR FIRST MISTAKE

-- BUT SO FAR, WE HAVE NOTHING MORE TO GO ON THAN AN OUT-OF-SERVICE PHONE NUMBER REGISTERED TO A FAKE ADDRESS IN *RIVER HEIGHTS*.
SO, FOR THE TIME BEING, WE'RE PUTTING *THAT* INVESTIGATION ON HOLD.
OUR CONCERN NOW IS WITH POSSIBLE CRIMINAL ACTIVITY BEHIND THE SCENES ON A POPULAR REALITY TV COMPETITION SHOW YOU MAY HAVE HEARD OF, CALLED "BREAK-UP."
"BREAK-UP?" I *LOVE* THAT SHOW!
BREAK-UP
JOE, PLEASE, I'M TRYING TO HEAR THIS.
ON "BREAK-UP," TEAMS OF TEENAGE *SIBLINGS* COMPETE AGAINST EACH OTHER IN WILD OBSTACLE COURSE TIME TRIALS.
WHICHEVER TEAM COMPLETES THE SERIES OF TRIALS THE FASTEST, WINS.
SIMPLE ENOUGH, IN THEORY, BUT IN *PRACTICE*, MAYBE *NOT* SO SIMPLE --

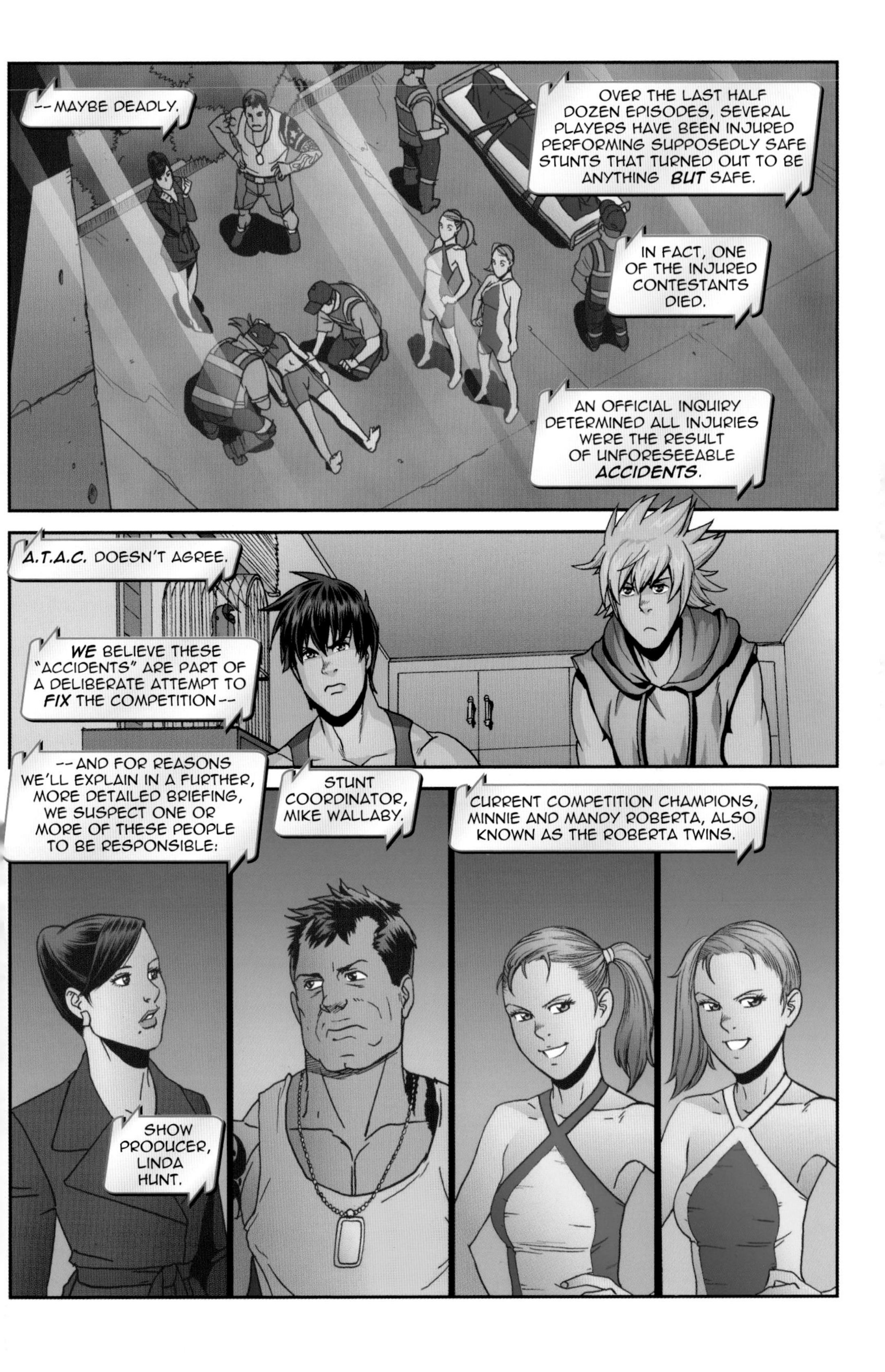
--MAYBE DEADLY.
OVER THE LAST HALF DOZEN EPISODES, SEVERAL PLAYERS HAVE BEEN INJURED PERFORMING SUPPOSEDLY SAFE STUNTS THAT TURNED OUT TO BE ANYTHING *BUT* SAFE.
IN FACT, ONE OF THE INJURED CONTESTANTS DIED.
AN OFFICIAL INQUIRY DETERMINED ALL INJURIES WERE THE RESULT OF UNFORESEEABLE *ACCIDENTS*.
A.T.A.C. DOESN'T AGREE.
WE BELIEVE THESE "ACCIDENTS" ARE PART OF A DELIBERATE ATTEMPT TO *FIX* THE COMPETITION--
--AND FOR REASONS WE'LL EXPLAIN IN A FURTHER, MORE DETAILED BRIEFING, WE SUSPECT ONE OR MORE OF THESE PEOPLE TO BE RESPONSIBLE:
SHOW PRODUCER, LINDA HUNT.
STUNT COORDINATOR, MIKE WALLABY.
CURRENT COMPETITION CHAMPIONS, MINNIE AND MANDY ROBERTA, ALSO KNOWN AS THE ROBERTA TWINS.

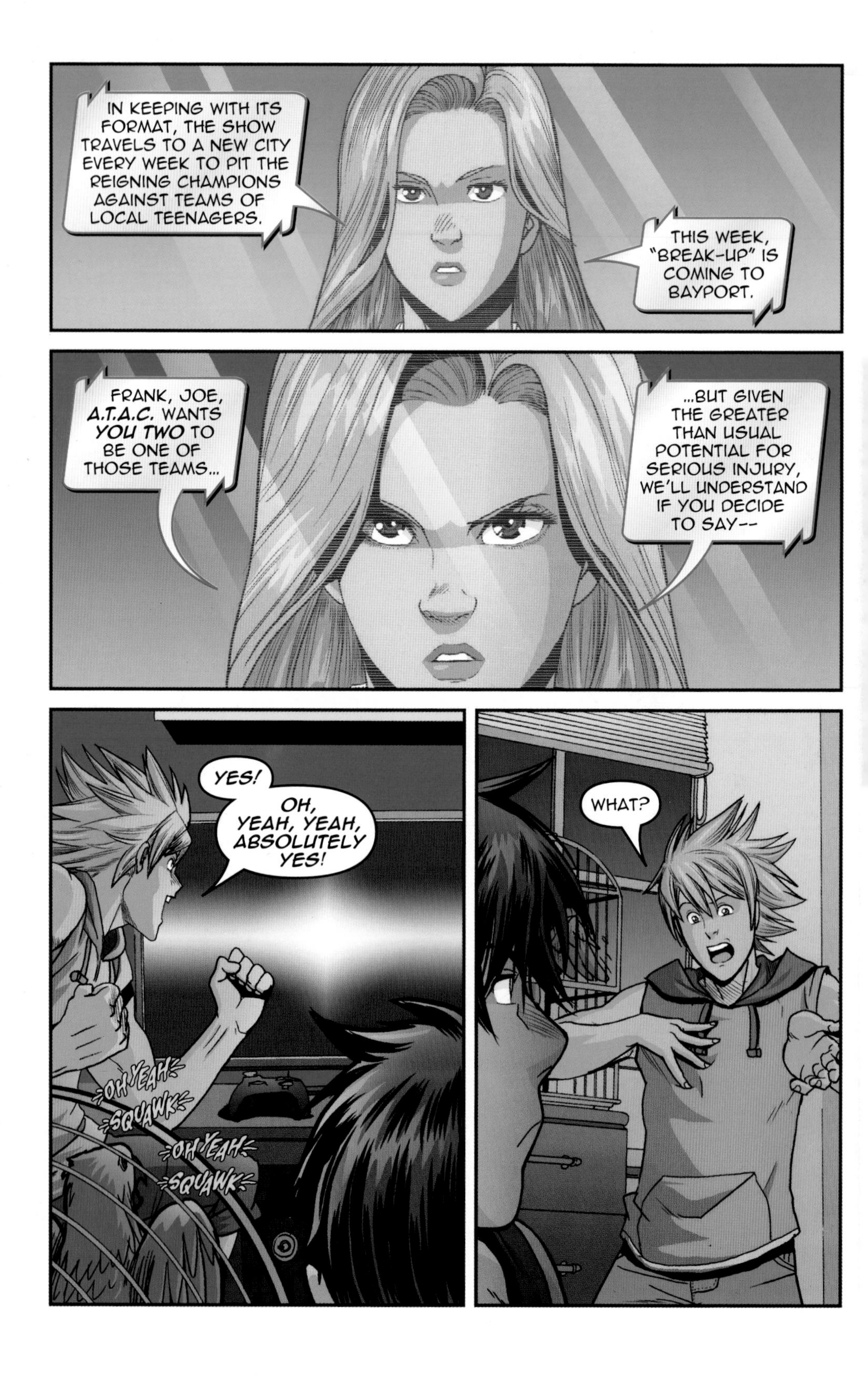
IN KEEPING WITH ITS FORMAT, THE SHOW TRAVELS TO A NEW CITY EVERY WEEK TO PIT THE REIGNING CHAMPIONS AGAINST TEAMS OF LOCAL TEENAGERS.
THIS WEEK, "BREAK-UP" IS COMING TO BAYPORT.
FRANK, JOE, A.T.A.C. WANTS *YOU TWO* TO BE ONE OF THOSE TEAMS...
...BUT GIVEN THE GREATER THAN USUAL POTENTIAL FOR SERIOUS INJURY, WE'LL UNDERSTAND IF YOU DECIDE TO SAY--
YES!
OH, YEAH, YEAH, ABSOLUTELY YES!
OH YEAH
SQUAWK
OH YEAH
SQUAWK
WHAT?

NOW.
TYPICAL JOE. ALWAYS READY TO RUSH INTO ACTION, WITHOUT A PLAN --
--JUST BARGE AHEAD AND HOPE FOR THE BEST.
THEN.
NO WONDER MOM'S ALWAYS WORRIED SOMETHING BAD IS GOING TO HAPPEN TO US.
COMPETING ON A REALITY TV GAME SHOW?
I DON'T KNOW, JOE. SOMETHING LIKE THAT, THE RISKS THOSE SHOWS MAKE YOU TAKE--
YOU BOYS MIGHT GET HURT.
"MIGHT" GET HURT?
LAURA, HAVE YOU SEEN "BREAK-UP?"
SHE KNOWS IF JOE ALWAYS GOT HIS WAY, WE'D PROBABLY BE DEAD BY NOW.

THEY'RE ACTUALLY PROUD OF THE FACT SOME OF THEIR CONTESTANTS HAVE LANDED IN THE HOSPITAL.
OF COURSE, IT DOESN'T HELP THAT AUNT TRUDY TENDS TOWARD THE HYSTERICAL.
LUCKILY, DAD KNOWS AT LEAST ONE OF US CAN BE TRUSTED NOT TO GO OFF HALF-COCKED.
LAURA, TRUDY, THE BOYS KNOW HOW TO TAKE CARE OF THEM-SELVES.
AND I'M SURE FRANK WILL MAKE CERTAIN THEY DON'T LET THEMSELVES GET TALKED INTO DOING ANYTHING TOO DANGEROUS.
YOU CAN COUNT ON ME, DAD.
I WISH I HAD YOUR CONFIDENCE, FENTON.
I JUST DON'T KNOW...
HMM.
WOULD YOU FEEL BETTER IF FRANK AND JOE HAD SOMEONE ALONG TO WATCH AFTER THEM?
DAD, YOU DON'T MEAN YOU--

GAME SHOWS AREN'T MY STYLE, SON.
YOU NEED A FRIEND YOUR AGE WHO'S AS CAUTIOUS AS YOUR MOM, AND WORRIES AS MUCH AS AUNT TRUDY.
KNOW ANYONE WHO FITS THAT DESCRIPTION?
DO WE!
GUYS, THIS IS SO GREAT!
"BREAK-UP" IS LIKE MY FAVORITE SHOW EVER!
WELL, SECOND FAVORITE, AFTER "BEST CHEF," BUT ONLY BECAUSE THAT ONE IS ABOUT FOOD.
AND YOU KNOW HOW I FEEL ABOUT FOOD.
PRETTY SURE EVERYBODY KNOWS HOW YOU FEEL ABOUT FOOD, CHET.

HE CAN ALSO BE A LITTLE... ENTHUSIASTIC.
BRINGING HIM ALONG PROBABLY COUNTS AS OUR FIRST MISTAKE...
SORRY, BOYS, THIS ENTRANCE IS FOR CONTESTANTS ONLY.
WE ARE CONTESTANTS. FRANK AND JOE HARDY.
THIS IS OUR FRIEND CHET MORTON.
YOU COULD SAY HE'S OUR PERSONAL ROOTING SECTION.
BREAK-UP

YEAH, MATE. AND WE COULD ALSO SAY HE'S NOT ALLOWED BACKSTAGE.
WHICH HE ISN'T. QUESTION OF SAFETY.
HEY, "MATE" -- HAND OFF THE CHEST. QUESTION OF PERSONAL SPACE.
NEVER MIND, MIKE. RULES ARE MADE TO BE BROKEN. LET THE KIDS THROUGH.
BUT, MS. HUNT --
I'M THE PRODUCER, REMEMBER? I DECIDE. I SAY LET THEM THROUGH.
RIGHT. ANYTHING HAPPENS, IT'S ON YOUR HEAD.
WHAT ELSE IS NEW?
GO ON IN THEN, MATES.
AND GOOD LUCK TO YOU.
YOU'LL NEED IT.

THAT GUY MIKE WALLABY ALMOST SOUNDS LIKE HE EXPECTS SOMETHING TO GO WRONG.
"ANYTHING HAPPENS, IT'S ON YOUR HEAD."
WHAT ABOUT THE PRODUCER, LINDA HUNT? "RULES ARE MADE TO BE BROKEN."
PRETTY CASUAL ATTITUDE FOR SUCH A DANGEROUS SHOW--
?
GOD WILL PUNISH YOU!
TELEVISION IS VANITY, COMPETITION FOR WORLDLY RECOGNITION IS AN AFFRONT TO THE LORD!
YOU'RE BUILDING A TOWER OF BABEL, AND GOD'S WRATH WILL SEND IT CRASHING DOWN!
SECURITY
WHO IS THAT, AND WHAT RUBBER-WALL ACADEMY LET HIM GRADUATE?
THAT IS JACOB "JUNIOR" GINGER, SON OF THE FAMOUS TV PREACHER, BIG JAKE GINGER...
... AND HE'S BEEN PROMISING DEATH AND DAMNATION TO EVERYBODY AROUND HERE ALL DAY.

CHAPTER THREE:
BABES IN TOYLAND
BRIAN? BELINDA? WHAT ARE YOU DOING HERE?
THEY KEEP THROWING HIM OUT, HE KEEPS TURNING UP AGAIN LIKE A BAD PENNY.
A LOT LIKE YOU TWO.
WHEN WE HEARD "BREAK-UP" WAS COMING TO TOWN AND WANTED A BROTHER-SISTER TEAM IN THE COMPETITION, BRIAN SAID, WHY SHOULDN'T IT BE US?
I ALMOST SAID NO TILL I FOUND OUT YOU AND JOE ARE PLAYING TOO.
HOW COULD I MISS THE CHANCE TO SPEND SOME QUALITY TIME WITH MY MAIN SQUEEZE?
FUN, RIGHT?

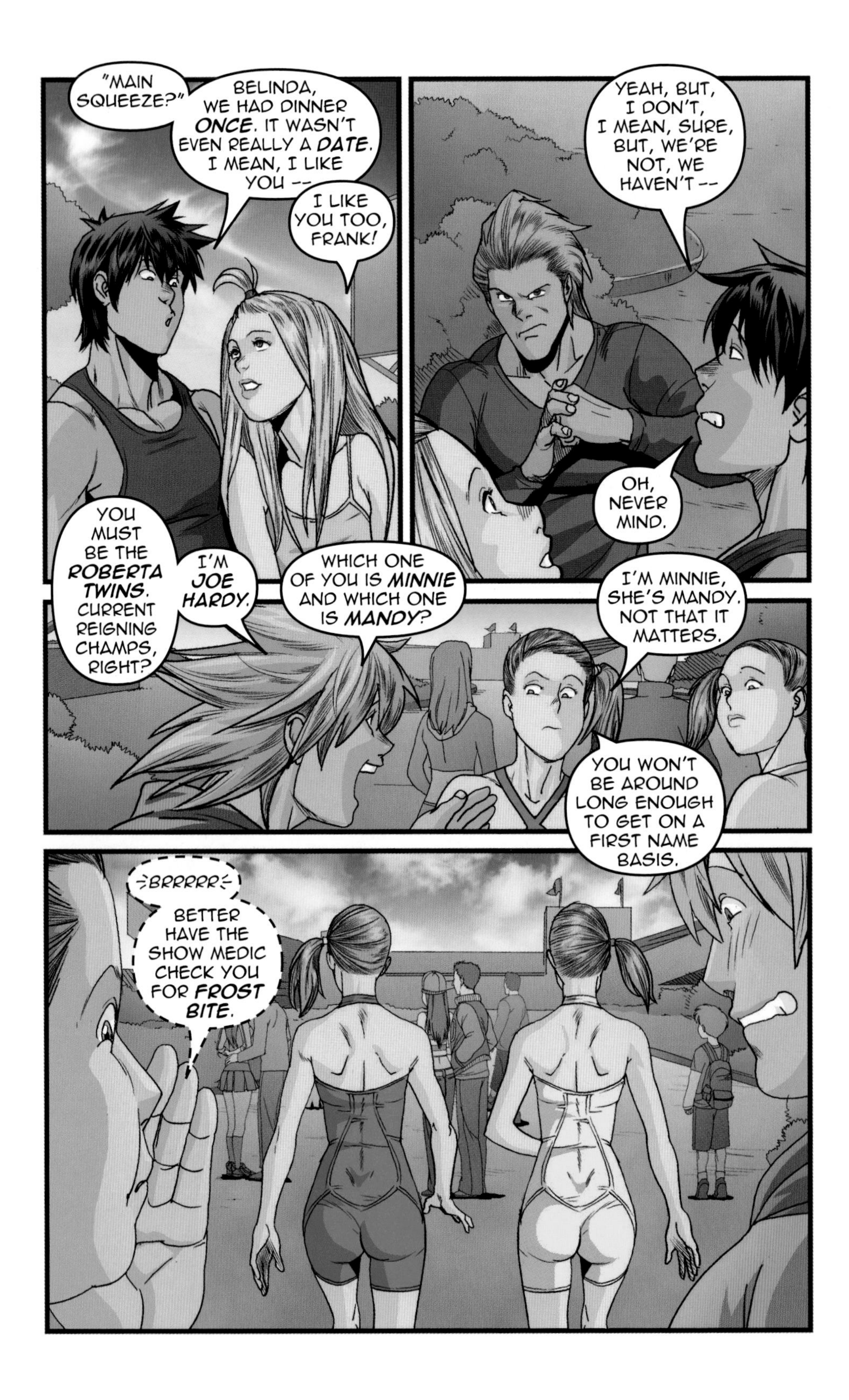
"MAIN SQUEEZE?"
BELINDA, WE HAD DINNER ONCE. IT WASN'T EVEN REALLY A DATE. I MEAN, I LIKE YOU --
I LIKE YOU TOO, FRANK!
YEAH, BUT, I DON'T, I MEAN, SURE, BUT, WE'RE NOT, WE HAVEN'T --
OH, NEVER MIND.
YOU MUST BE THE ROBERTA TWINS. CURRENT REIGNING CHAMPS, RIGHT?
I'M JOE HARDY.
WHICH ONE OF YOU IS MINNIE AND WHICH ONE IS MANDY?
I'M MINNIE, SHE'S MANDY. NOT THAT IT MATTERS.
YOU WON'T BE AROUND LONG ENOUGH TO GET ON A FIRST NAME BASIS.
BRRRRR
BETTER HAVE THE SHOW MEDIC CHECK YOU FOR FROST BITE.

ONCE THEY GET TO KNOW ME, THEY'LL WARM UP.
OH, SURE. MAYBE FROM SUB-ZERO ALL THE WAY UP TO FREEZING.
JOE, CHET--
WATCH OUT!!
KRASSH!!!
SWEET MOTHER OF MERCY, YOU BOYOS ALL RIGHT?
YEAH, THANKS TO FRANK!
I SAW THAT SCAFFOLDING START TO TOPPLE, JUST REACTED--
WHEW! LUCKY YOU HAPPENED TO BE LOOKING OUR WAY.

LUCK HAD NOTHING TO DO WITH IT, LITTLE BROTHER.
I WAS PAYING ATTENTION. YOU WEREN'T.
SOME GUY FORGETS TO WELD A FEW RIVETS AND THAT'S MY FAULT?
NO, BUT IF YOU'D BEEN WATCHING YOUR BACK, INSTEAD OF OBSESSING OVER A PAIR OF GIRLS WHO DIDN'T HAPPEN TO FIND YOU ABSOLUTELY FASCINATING--
NOT A "PAIR OF GIRLS," FRANK. THE ROBERTA TWINS ARE SUSPECTS, REMEMBER?
OH, SO YOU WERE FLIRTING WITH THEM BECAUSE THEY WERE SUSPECTS?
OR BECAUSE THEY HAPPEN TO BE PRETTY AND THE SUSPECT PART WAS JUST A BONUS?
KNOW YOUR PROBLEM, FRANK?
YOU THINK THE ONLY IDEAS THAT MATTER ARE THE IDEAS YOU COME UP WITH.
AT LEAST I HAVE IDEAS!
BROTHER, THAT'S ALL YOU HAVE!

UH, GUYS... ARE YOU OKAY?
YEAH, SURE, WE'RE FINE.
THE QUESTION IS -- WHAT HAPPENED TO THAT SCAFFOLDING? WHY DID IT COLLAPSE LIKE THAT?
WISH I KNEW, MATES.
I KEEP A CLOSE WATCH ON CONSTRUCTION -- THAT'S MY JOB -- AND I COULDA SWORN THAT SCAFFOLD WAS SAFE AS HOUSES.
ACCIDENTS HAPPEN, MIKE.
THAT'S WHY WE HAVE INSURANCE.
ARE YOU KIDDING ME?
WHAT IF THAT HAPPENED WHILE YOU WERE TAPING A SHOW? SOMEBODY COULD'VE BEEN KILLED.
HEY, YOUR PARENTS SIGNED A RELEASE. WOULD'VE MADE GREAT TV.
BUT SINCE NO ONE WAS HURT, WHY WORRY ABOUT IT?
GET THEM READY, MIKE. WE START TAPING IN AN HOUR.

JOE... LOOK AT LINDA HUNT'S HAND...
DO YOU SEE WHAT I SEE?
YOU MEAN THAT GREASE SMUDGE ON HER HAND?
SOMEBODY MADE THAT SCAFFOLDING CRASH.
WHOEVER DID IT MIGHT HAVE GOTTEN THEIR HANDS DIRTY.
ONE OF US OUGHT TO KEEP AN EYE ON MS. GREASE-MONKEY PRODUCER LADY.
I NOMI-NATE ME.
GUYS, THEY WANT YOU TO GET READY--
HARDYS! OVER HERE OR YOU'RE OUT OF THE GAME!
STALL THE MAN, FRANK.
I'LL CATCH UP WITH YOU IN A FEW MINUTES.
JOE-- NO--

I HATE WHEN HE DOES THAT.
WHAT'S UP WITH YOU GUYS, FRANK?
IT FEELS LIKE YOU'RE AT EACH OTHER'S THROATS ALL THE TIME LATELY.
TELL ME ABOUT IT.
EVERYTHING JOE SAYS RUBS ME THE WRONG WAY. EVERYTHING I SAY RUBS HIM THE WRONG WAY.
BUT, ASK ME WHY, AND I DON'T KNOW.
MAYBE YOU GUYS ARE JUST TOGETHER TOO MUCH.
YOU LIVE TOGETHER, YOU GO TO SCHOOL TOGETHER, YOU SOLVE MYSTERIES TOGETHER.
IF YOU WEREN'T A LITTLE SICK OF EACH OTHER AFTER ALL THAT, YOU WOULDN'T BE HUMAN.
YOU'RE PROBABLY RIGHT.
BUT WE'RE THE HARDY BOYS. WE'RE A TEAM.
CAN'T HAVE ONE OF US WITHOUT THE --
OH. WOW.
WORDS. OUT OF MY MOUTH. YOU TOOK.

CHAPTER FOUR:
DIRTY WORK
LOOK... AT ALL... THESE TOYS.
FORGET THE TOYS.
LOOK AT THE BABES.
FRANK! AREN'T THESE OUTFITS CUTE?
I FEEL LIKE A JAMES BOND GIRL.

YEAH, MAYBE IF BOND GIRLS WERE SOFT AND DUMPY.
WE ARE SO GOING TO EAT YOUR LUNCH, GIRLY-GIRL.
YOU AND YOUR BROTHER AND YOUR BOYFRIEND AND YOUR BOYFRIEND'S BROTHER.
AND SPEAKING OF YOUR BOYFRIEND'S BROTHER -- WHERE'S HE HIDING HIMSELF?
YOU DO KNOW IF BLONDIE ISN'T HERE BY SHOWTIME HE AND TALL-DARK-AND-DUMB AUTOMATICALLY LOSE.
THE ROBERTA GIRL'S RIGHT, HARDY.
NO SHOW, NO GO.

"AND THAT'S MY PROBLEM WITH JOE, IN A NUTSHELL.
"WE'RE SUPPOSED TO BE A TEAM, BUT LATELY HE'S BEEN PLAYING SOLO."
THEN.
NOW.
MY PROBLEM WITH FRANK IS, FOR HIM, EVERYTHING IS ABOUT TEAM WORK.
AND LOOK WHERE THAT'S GOTTEN US.
HE DOESN'T UNDERSTAND DETECTING DEPENDS ON INSTINCT AND INITIATIVE.
THEN.
"THAT'S WHY I FOLLOWED LINDA HUNT TO HER OFFICE TRAILER IN THE BACK STAGE AREA.
"INSTINCT AND INITIATIVE."

HEY, YOU -- "JUNIOR" --
THAT'S BACKSTAGE FOR THE SPINNING BARREL STUNT.
NO ONE ALLOWED EXCEPT SHOW PERSONNEL.
S-SORRY...
I WAS LOOKING FOR THE EXIT AND GOT TURNED AROUND...
KEEP TURNING.
IT'S RIGHT BEHIND YOU.
WELL, WELL. TSK, TSK. GUESS SOMEBODY FORGOT INTERNET SAFETY RULE NOS. 1 AND 2.
"NEVER LEAVE YOUR WEB BROWSER OPEN --"
"--AND ALWAYS CLEAR YOUR HISTORY CACHE."
HUH. NOW LOOK AT THAT.
WHEN LINDA HUNT SAID THE SHOW WAS COVERED BY INSURANCE, SHE WASN'T KIDDING.

WAIT TILL FRANK HEARS ABOUT THIS.
ASSUMING HE CAN STOP LECTURING ME LONG ENOUGH TO LET ME TELL HIM.
MS. HUNT. WE'RE READY TO GO IN FIVE.
IN CASE YOU FORGOT, MY STUNT TEAM STILL NEEDS THE LOCK CODE FOR THE ULTIMATE CHALLENGE SET.
NOBODY GOES NEAR THAT SET TILL WE'RE READY TO SHOOT ON IT.

THAT'S CRAZY, WOMAN.
HOW CAN I KEEP PEOPLE SAFE IF YOU WON'T LET ME DO MY JOB?
AND MY JOB IS TO MAKE SURE THE ULTIMATE CHALLENGE STAYS A SURPRISE FOR THE VIEWERS.
LIVE WITH IT, MIKE.
OR I'LL FIND ANOTHER STUNT COORDINATOR WHO CAN.
"I FIGURED FRANK WOULD WANT TO HEAR WHAT I FOUND OUT AS SOON AS I CAUGHT UP WITH HIM.
"I FIGURED WRONG."
FRANK, LISTEN--
NOT NOW, JOE!
THE GAME'S ABOUT TO START!
YEAH, BUT--
C'MON!
STAFF

NO BUTS. MOVE.
=WOOFF!=
WHAT KIND OF STUNT IS THIS, ANYWAY?
IF YOU'D BEEN HERE FOR PREP, YOU'D KNOW.
WELL, I WASN'T, SO JUST TELL ME, FRANK.
WHAT EXACTLY AM I SUPPOSED TO DO IN HERE?
EASY.
STAY UP!
WHHHHAOOOAOAOO
RRRRRUMBBLE

RRRROMMMMMBLE
OKAY. GIVE ME CAMERA THREE ON THE MAIN MONITOR.
GOOD. NOW CUT TO CAMERA ONE.
PAN CAMERA FOUR.
BARRY, WHAT'S WITH THE SOUND FEED? TOO MUCH VIBRATION IN THE OUTPUT.
TOGGLE BACK ON THE BASS, ALL RIGHT?
RRRROMMMMMBLE
THAT VIBRATION ISN'T PART OF THE SOUND FEED, SIR.
IT'S COMING FROM OUTSIDE!
THE BARREL--
RRROMMMMBLE
--IT'S OUT OF CONTROL!
OHMIGOSH!

JOE, SOMETHING'S WRONG! THE BARREL'S TURNING TOO FAST!
NO, REALLY, YOU THINK?
EEEEE!
DON'T WORRY, BELINDA, I'VE GOT YOU --
UNNHGH!
SOME-BODY HIT THE SHUT-OFF!
ANDY, BILL, TOM -- ANYONE -- ANSWER ME!
PLEASE TELL ME YOU'RE RECORDING THIS!
MS. HUNT, ARE YOU INSANE? THOSE KIDS ARE GOING TO GET KILLED!
IF ANYONE GETS KILLED, I WANT IT RECORDED.
THE NETWORK WANTS REALITY, WE'LL GIVE THEM REALITY!
FRANK, JOE! WHAT CAN I DO? HOW CAN I HELP? GUYS, PLEASE, TELL ME!

CHET
SWITCH
BEHIND
YOU
OHMANIHOPETHISWORKS!
OOOOF
UNNGHH
UMHPH
EEEEP
AWWK

ARE YOU KIDS ALL RIGHT?
I THINK MINNIE'S HURT.
HOW COULD THIS HAPPEN? WHERE WAS YOUR SAFETY CREW?
SOMEBODY **TEXTED** THEM, SAID I WANTED 'EM OFF THE SET.
WHEN I FIND OUT **WHO** --
YOU THERE! GET THE **PARAMEDICS!** THIS GIRL NEEDS HELP!
FRANK, WE NEED TO TALK.
NOT NOW, JOE, WE HAVE TO --
I SAID WE NEED TO TALK!

CHAPTER FIVE:
FLYING DUECES
OKAY, I ADMIT IT, I WAS ANGRY.
"BUT I FELT LIKE I HAD A GOOD REASON."
YOU NEVER LISTEN TO ME.
I TRIED TO TELL YOU BEFORE WE GOT IN THAT BARREL -- LINDA HUNT HAS THIS SHOW INSURED FOR A FORTUNE.
SHE DOESN'T NEED IT TO BE A HIT --
IN FACT, IT'S PROBABLY WORTH MORE TO HER IF SOMEBODY GETS KILLED AND IT'S CANCELLED!
GET YOUR FINGER OUT OF MY CHEST, JOE.
AND TRY TO REMEMBER, LITTLE BROTHER, WE NEED MORE THAN MOTIVE TO PROVE SOMEONE'S COMMITTED A CRIME.
"TRUTH IS, THOUGH, I DIDN'T REALLY NEED A REASON. LATELY, WHENEVER I'M AROUND FRANK, MY INTERNAL THERMOMETER JUST SEEMS STUCK IN THE RED ZONE."

WHAT ABOUT MEANS AND OPPORTUNITY?
FOR EXAMPLE, WAS LINDA HUNT THE ONLY SUSPECT WITH ACCESS TO THE BARREL CONTROLS?
WELL, NO-- "JUNIOR" GINGER WAS SNEAKING AROUND--
--BUT THE POINT IS--
--THE POINT IS, YOU'RE JUMPING TO A CON-CLUSION.
JUST. LIKE. ALWAYS.
DON'T POKE ME, FRANK.
WHY NOT? WHAT'LL YOU DO, HIT ME?
THAT'S HOW YOU SOLVE ALL YOUR PROBLEMS, ISN'T IT?
WITH YOUR FISTS INSTEAD OF YOUR HEAD?
DO. NOT. POKE. ME.
POIK

YAAAAAHHH!
KLIK

"LIKE FRANK REMINDED ME WHEN WE WOKE UP, WE WERE LUCKY WE WEREN'T KILLED."
THEN.
NOW.
THOUGH I GUESS "LUCKY" IS WHAT YOU'D CALL A RELATIVE TERM.
SO, AH, BRO...
ANY IDEA HOW WE GET OUT OF THIS?

OH, SO **NOW** YOU WANT MY INPUT.
WELL, AS IT TURNS OUT, I **DO** HAVE AN IDEA.
KICK ME.

TEMPTING AS THAT SOUNDS -- HUH?
JUST DO IT, OKAY?
OKAY, OKAY, BUT IF I LEAVE BRUISES, REMEMBER TO TELL MOM THIS WAS YOUR IDEA.
UMPHH
GOOD.
FIRST YOU KICK --
OWWHH
-- THEN I KICK --
-- THEN YOU KICK -- HARD--
UMOWPPH

-- AND I KICK BACK HARDER!
YOWWW
RATTLTTLTLETTLELE
UMPH
YOWCH
KAKLANG

YOU ENJOYED THAT.
SO DID YOU.
YEAH, BUT IT WAS YOUR IDEA.
REALLY? ARE WE REALLY GOING TO START THIS AGAIN NOW?
NAH, LET'S SAVE IT FOR LATER.
AFTER WE NAB THE PERSON WHO TRIED TO KILL US.
WHICH COULD BE ANYONE.
ACTUALLY, NO, IT COULDN'T BE JUST "ANYONE."
FROM WHAT I HEARD EARLIER, ONLY ONE PERSON HAD THE ACCESS CODE FOR THE LOCKED DOOR TO THIS STAGE SET, THE "ULTIMATE CHALLENGE."
WHO?
FRANK, JOE -- YOU'RE OKAY!
WHEN YOU WENT MISSING, MR. WALLABY SHUT DOWN THE SHOW.
WE LOOKED FOR YOU EVERYWHERE, FRANK --

-- UNTIL "JUNIOR" GINGER HERE MENTIONED HE SAW SOMEONE HE COULDN'T RECOGNIZE COMING OUT OF THE ULTIMATE CHALLENGE SET.
OH, YEAH? AND WHAT WERE YOU DOING BACK HERE, "JUNIOR?"
SABOTAGING ANOTHER STUNT?
JOE SAW YOU SNEAKING AROUND THE BARREL CONTROLS BEFORE THE STUNT WENT WRONG --
MIKE WALLABY. YOU'RE IN CHARGE OF SAFETY ON SET.
THEN IT MUST'VE BEEN YOU WHO ALMOST ELECTROCUTED US IN THE HOPSHOCK CHALLENGE SET.
FRANK --
UH, FRANK--
WHAT?
YEAH, I'M THE ONE WHO CAUGHT HIM. WHOEVER BROKE THE SAFETY LOCK ON THE BARREL CONTROL, IT WASN'T "JUNIOR" HERE.
AFTER I THREW HIM OUT, I MADE SURE HE DIDN'T DAMAGE ANYTHING.
REMEMBER I SAID ONLY ONE PERSON HAS THE ACCESS CODE TO THE ULTIMATE CHALLENGE SET?
THAT PERSON ISN'T MIKE WALLABY.
IT'S LINDA HUNT.

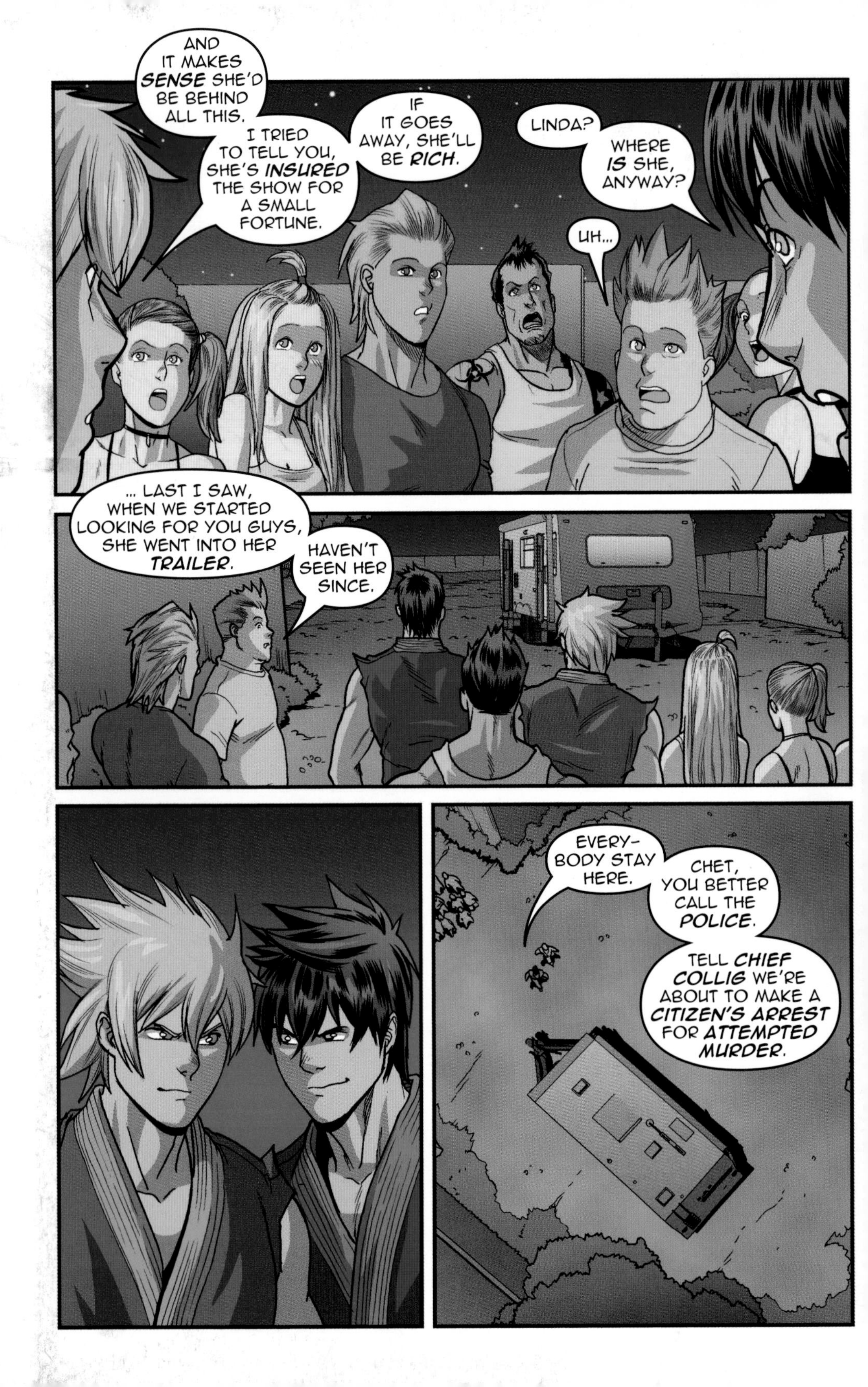
AND IT MAKES SENSE SHE'D BE BEHIND ALL THIS.
I TRIED TO TELL YOU, SHE'S INSURED THE SHOW FOR A SMALL FORTUNE.
IF IT GOES AWAY, SHE'LL BE RICH.
LINDA?
WHERE IS SHE, ANYWAY?
UH...
... LAST I SAW, WHEN WE STARTED LOOKING FOR YOU GUYS, SHE WENT INTO HER TRAILER.
HAVEN'T SEEN HER SINCE.
EVERY-BODY STAY HERE.
CHET, YOU BETTER CALL THE POLICE.
TELL CHIEF COLLIG WE'RE ABOUT TO MAKE A CITIZEN'S ARREST FOR ATTEMPTED MURDER.

MS. HUNT?
MS. HUNT, WE KNOW WHAT YOU'VE DONE AND WHY YOU DID IT.
THE POLICE ARE ON THE WAY.
MS. HUNT?

WHOA.
DIDN'T SEE THAT COMING.

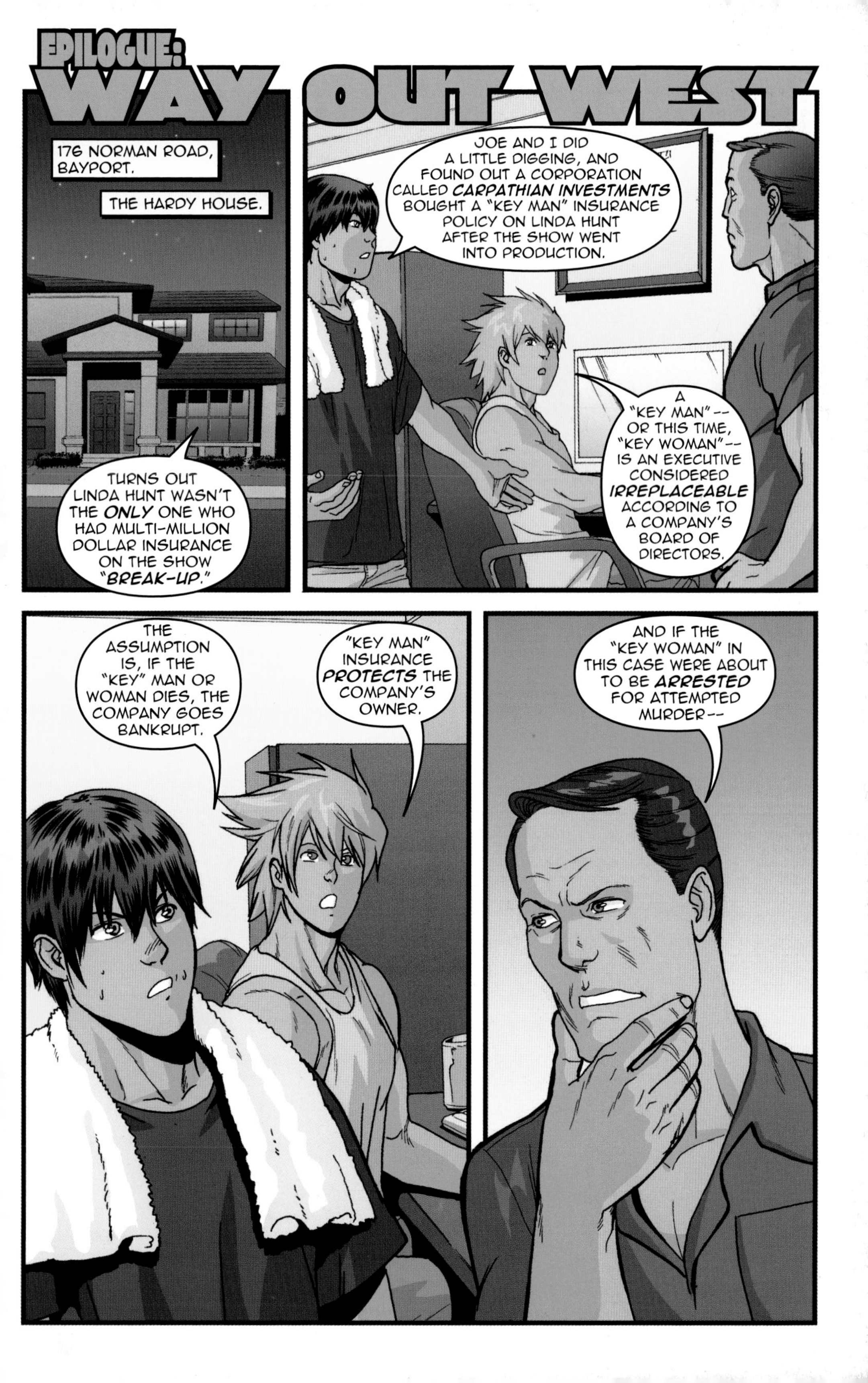
EPILOGUE:
WAY OUT WEST
176 NORMAN ROAD, BAYPORT.
THE HARDY HOUSE.
TURNS OUT LINDA HUNT WASN'T THE ONLY ONE WHO HAD MULTI-MILLION DOLLAR INSURANCE ON THE SHOW "BREAK-UP."
JOE AND I DID A LITTLE DIGGING, AND FOUND OUT A CORPORATION CALLED CARPATHIAN INVESTMENTS BOUGHT A "KEY MAN" INSURANCE POLICY ON LINDA HUNT AFTER THE SHOW WENT INTO PRODUCTION.
A "KEY MAN" -- OR THIS TIME, "KEY WOMAN"-- IS AN EXECUTIVE CONSIDERED IRREPLACEABLE ACCORDING TO A COMPANY'S BOARD OF DIRECTORS.
THE ASSUMPTION IS, IF THE "KEY" MAN OR WOMAN DIES, THE COMPANY GOES BANKRUPT.
"KEY MAN" INSURANCE PROTECTS THE COMPANY'S OWNER.
AND IF THE "KEY WOMAN" IN THIS CASE WERE ABOUT TO BE ARRESTED FOR ATTEMPTED MURDER--

--KILLING HER TO COLLECT THE INSURANCE WOULD BE ONE SURE WAY FOR AN INVESTOR TO GET HIS, HER, OR ITS MONEY BACK.
FENTON, BOYS -- DINNER TIME.
FRANK AND JOE, DON'T KEEP YOUR MOTHER WAITING!
WHICH BEGS THE QUESTION -- WHO OR WHAT IS CARPATHIAN INVESTMENTS?
SO FAR AS WE CAN FIND OUT, NOBODY KNOWS.
JOE'S EXAGGERATING, BUT NOT BY MUCH.
CARPATHIAN IS A PRIVATE HOLDING COMPANY, OWNED BY A SHELL CORPORATION, WHOLLY CONTROLLED BY AN INVESTMENT FUND ORGANIZED AS A BLIND TRUST--
-- REGISTERED ANONYMOUSLY IN THE CAYMAN ISLANDS.
SO, YOU HAVE NO LEADS?
NO WAY TO FIND OUT WHO OWNS CARPATHIAN INVESTMENTS, WHO KILLED LINDA HUNT?
ACTUALLY, WE DO HAVE ONE LEAD.
A PHONE NUMBER ON CARPATHIAN'S CAYMAN ISLAND INCORPORATION PAPERS.

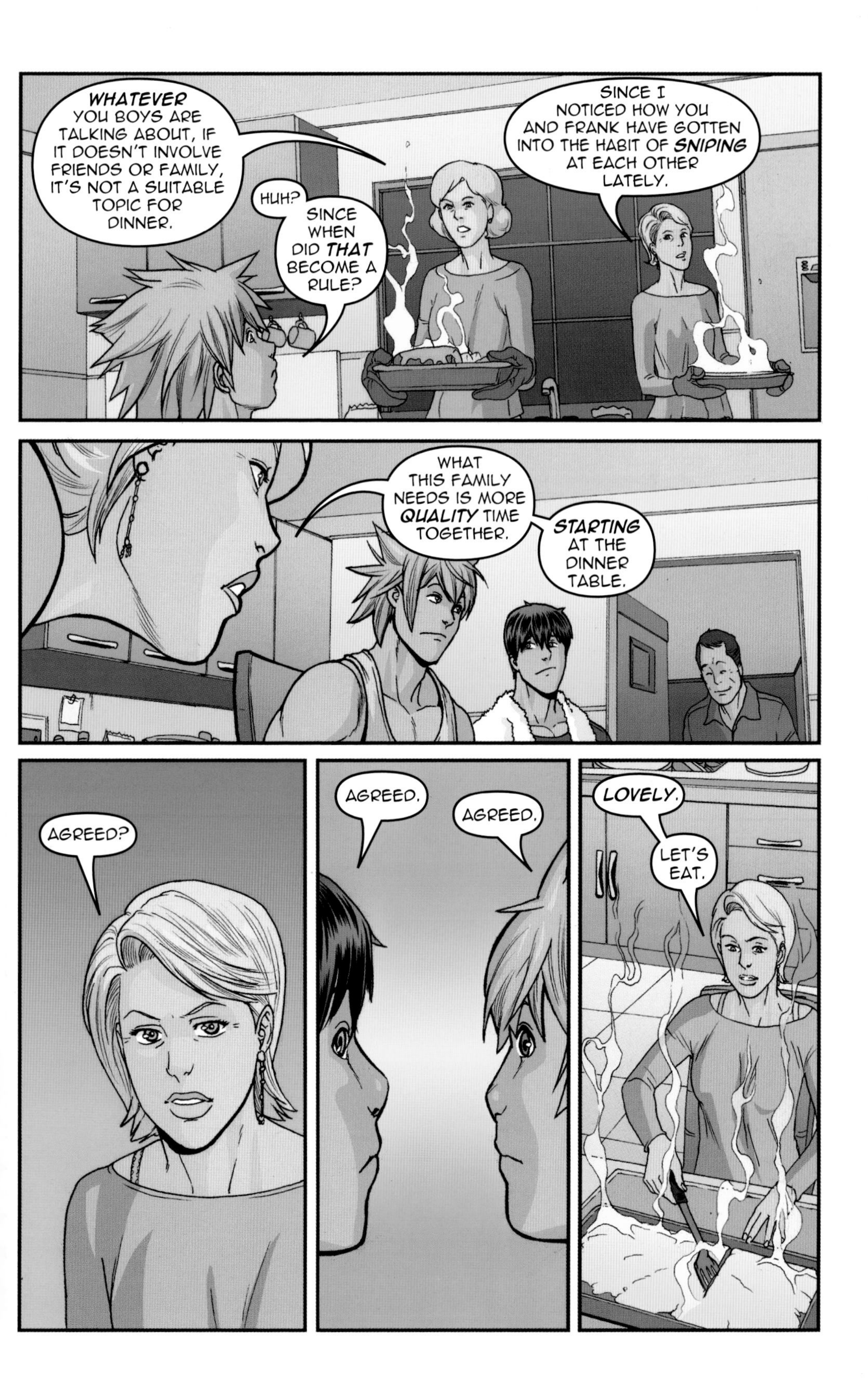
WHATEVER YOU BOYS ARE TALKING ABOUT, IF IT DOESN'T INVOLVE FRIENDS OR FAMILY, IT'S NOT A SUITABLE TOPIC FOR DINNER.
HUH?
SINCE WHEN DID THAT BECOME A RULE?
SINCE I NOTICED HOW YOU AND FRANK HAVE GOTTEN INTO THE HABIT OF SNIPING AT EACH OTHER LATELY.
WHAT THIS FAMILY NEEDS IS MORE QUALITY TIME TOGETHER.
STARTING AT THE DINNER TABLE.
AGREED?
AGREED.
AGREED.
LOVELY.
LET'S EAT.

LATER.
YOUR MOTHER'S RIGHT, YOU KNOW.
YOU BOYS HAVE BEEN AT EACH OTHER'S THROATS A LOT LATELY.
WELL, IT'S JOE'S FAULT --
MY FAULT? YOU'RE THE ONE WHO --
ENOUGH.
THIS PHONE NUMBER YOU MENTIONED. HAVE YOU TRACED IT?
WE DID.
IT'S THE SAME PHONE NUMBER USED BY THOSE THUGS WHO TRIED TO ROB THE BAYPORT MUSEUM USING A ZOMBIE CRAWL FOR COVER.*
REGISTERED TO A PHONY ADDRESS WAY OUT WEST IN RIVER HEIGHTS.
*SEE HARDY BOYS THE NEW CASE FILES #1.
I'LL LET A.T.A.C. KNOW WHAT YOU'VE LEARNED, AND WHAT HAPPENS NEXT IS UP TO THEM, BUT IF I WERE YOU, I'D CLEAR MY SCHEDULE FOR THE NEXT FEW WEEKENDS.
PROVIDED YOU CAN MANAGE IT WITHOUT STRANGLING EACH OTHER...
I'D SAY YOUR NEXT STEP IN SOLVING THIS MYSTERY IS A VISIT WITH YOUR FRIEND NANCY DREW IN RIVER HEIGHTS.
TO BE CONTINUED -- IN NANCY DREW THE NEW CASE FILES #3!

WATCH OUT FOR PAPERCUTZ

Welcome to the second awesome volume of the all-new THE HARDY BOYS The New Case Files graphic novel series! I'm retired A.T.A.C. agent Jim Salicrup, Editor-in-Chief of Papercutz, publisher of graphic novels for all-ages. Generally, this page is devoted to getting you all the latest news from Papercutz—letting you know what's going on in many of the other great Papercutz graphic novels. Since there's so much to tell, we're going to run through all the exciting announcements as fast as we can, and try to squeeze as much as possible onto this page!

BIONICLE #9 "The Fall of Atero" – It's "The BIONICLE Glatorian saga!" This is perhaps the most action-packed graphic novel series ever published by Papercutz! If you're familiar with the BIONICLE, but never seen the comics—what are you waiting for?! Written by Greg Farshtey, illustrated by Pop Mhan.

CLASSICS ILLUSTRATED #12 "The Island of Dr. Moreau" – This is the graphic novel series that takes stories by the world's greatest authors and adapts them into comics. H. G. Wells's tragic tale of monstrous mutants is brought to dark life by writer Steven Grant, and artist Eric Vincent.

DISNEY ADVENTURES #5 "Tinker Bell and the Pirate Adventure" – Now in the same bigger format as HARDY BOYS THE NEW CASE FILES! Think life is easy in Never Land? Then you've probably forgot all about Captain Hook! He's back, along with his pirates, to disrupt the lives of Tinker Bell, Terence, and the other fairies. Giulia Conti, Augusto Machetto, & Paola Mulazzi, writers; Gianluca Barone,Andrea Greppi, Elisabetta Melaranci, & Emilio Urbano, artists.

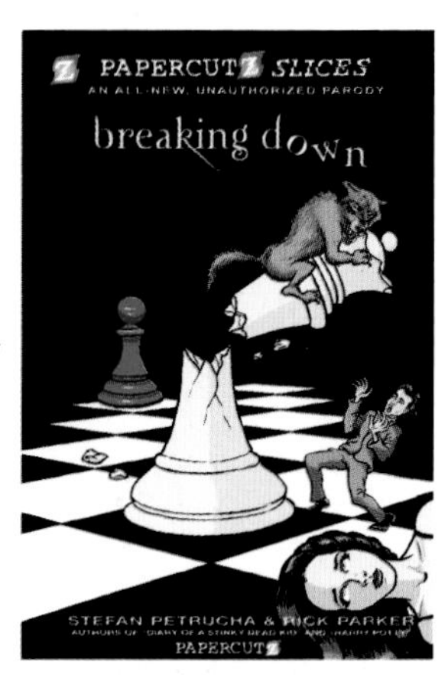

GERONIMO STILTON #7 "Dinosaurs in Action" – Geronimo and friends travel all the way back in time to the Cretaceous Period to rescue Professor Von Volt from the Pirate Cats! If that wasn't tough enough, a few dinosaurs make matters positively dangerous!

TALES FROM THE CRYPT #9 "Wickeder" – Glugg, the Stinky Dead Kid is back in an all-new story by Margo Kinney-Petrucha & Stefan Petrucha, writers; Diego Jourdan, artist. Plus "Kill, Baby, Kill!" by Scott Lobdell, writer; James Romberger & Marguerite Van Cook, artists. Gross and creepy comics with a twisted sense of humor!

PAPERCUTZ SLICES #2 "Breaking Down" – The unofficial parody of the Twilight series, as sliced up by Maia Kinney-Petrucha, Stefan Petrucha, writers; Rick Parker, artist.

THE SMURFS #5 "The Smurfs and the Egg" – A magic egg, one that can grant any wish, throws the Smurf Village into turmoil! If that wasn't enough, the evil sorcerer Gargamel has concocted a potion that turns him into "The Fake Smurf"! Yvan Delporte & Peyo, writers; Peyo, artist.

And if that's not enough graphic novels to keep you entertained 'till Summer, you must check out NANCY DREW The New Case Files #2 "Vampire Slayer" Part Two (Check out the preview on the following pages)! Why? The answer is that parts one and two of "Vampire Slayer," as well as THE HARDY BOYS The New Case Files #1 and #2 all lead into NANCY DREW The New Case Files #3 "Together with The Hardy Boys"!

Yes, at long last, due to popular demand, Nancy Drew and The The Hardy Boys finally team-up in a graphic novel! But it's a team-up like you've never seen before—Frank and Joe Hardy no longer want to work together, and Ned Nickerson has left Nancy Drew. With all these personal conflicts how can the teen detectives hope to solve one of their biggest mysteries ever? Whatever you do, don't miss NANCY DREW The New Case Files #3 "Together with The Hardy Boys," written by Gerry Conway and drawn by Sho Murase! Be sure to check www.papercutz.com for further details.

Till then, watch out for Papercutz!

Thanks, Jim

Available Now . . .

NANCY DREW THE NEW CASE FILES
002 Based on the series by Carolyn Keene Girl Detective®
VAMPIRE SLAYER PART TWO
By Petrucha, Kinney & Murase
PAPERCUTZ

Nancy Drew must stop a woman determined to destroy a vampire -- Gregor Coffson! But why? Has the Girl Detective fallen under the vampire's spell? Don't miss the shock-filled conclusion to "Vampire Slayer."

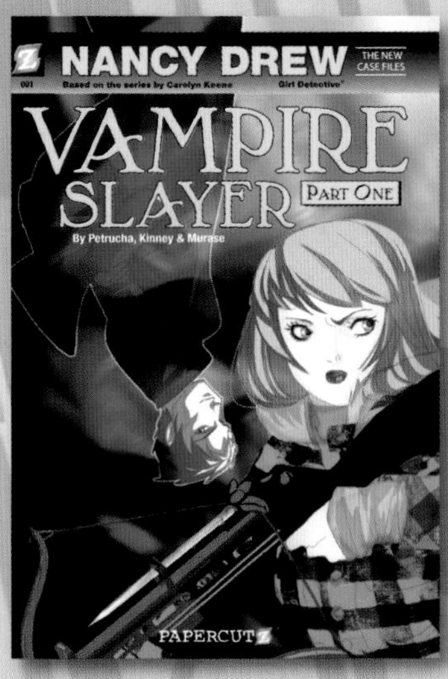

Still available:
"Vampire Slayer" Part I!

6x9, 64 pages, full-color. $6.99 PB, $10.99 HC. On sale at booksellers everywhere.
Or order from us. Please add $4.00 postage and handling plus $1.00 for each additional book. Please make check payable to NBM Publishing. Send to: PAPERCUTZ, 1200 Country Rd. Rte. 523, Flemington, NJ, 08822. (1-800-886-1223)

www.papercutz.com

Special preview of NANCY DREW
The New Case Files #2 "Vampire Slayer" Part Two!

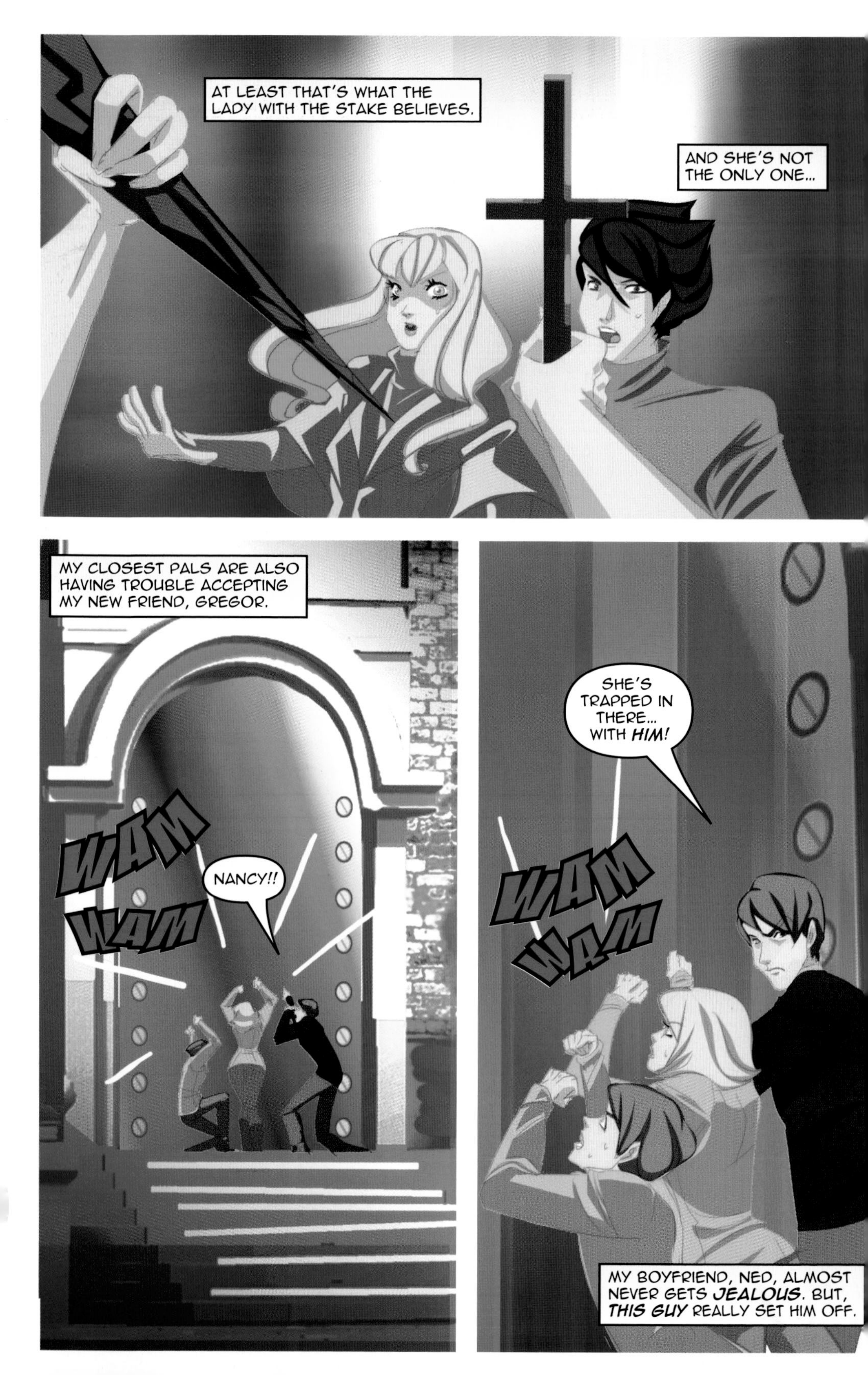
AT LEAST THAT'S WHAT THE LADY WITH THE STAKE BELIEVES.
AND SHE'S NOT THE ONLY ONE...
MY CLOSEST PALS ARE ALSO HAVING TROUBLE ACCEPTING MY NEW FRIEND, GREGOR.
WAM
WAM
NANCY!!
SHE'S TRAPPED IN THERE... WITH HIM!
WAM
WAM
MY BOYFRIEND, NED, ALMOST NEVER GETS JEALOUS. BUT, THIS GUY REALLY SET HIM OFF.

BRAINWASHED BY VAMPIRE MOVIE MANIA, MY BEST FRIENDS, BESS AND GEORGE HAD SUSPICIONS THAT MADE THEM BREAK INTO GREGOR'S RENTED ESTATE!
ALL RIGHT. SO, I MAY HAVE BROKEN INTO THIS PLACE MYSELF A WHILE BACK, TO INVESTIGATE A MAGICIAN RENTING IT AT THE TIME.* BUT, IT WAS STILL CRAZY RECKLESS OF THEM!
SLAM
TO BE FAIR, THEY HAD A MINUTE WHEN THEY SEEMED TO BE COMING TO THEIR SENSES...
*SEE NANCY DREW GRAPHIC NOVEL #14 "SLEIGHT OF DAN."
...UNTIL THE HOUSE LOCKED OUT ALL RATIONAL THOUGHT!
HE'S GOING TO SUCK NANCY'S BLOOD!!
HE'LL MAKE HER LIKE HIM!!
OR WORSE!!
WHAT COULD BE WORSE?!

I'D BEEN IN SOME FREAKY PREDICAMENTS IN MY TIME, BUT THIS WAS LOOKING LIKE THE STRANGEST YET!

I THINK I'M GOING TO FAINT!

GREGOR!

NANCY, DON'T LET HER-- UNGH!

MY... STOMACH! I NEED... I NEED TO... DRINK!
NO! RELEASE HER! I WON'T LET YOU DRINK HER BLOOD!
DON'T YOU SEE! HE'S SICK! THERE'S NO SUCH THING AS VAMPIRES!
THERE IS! GREGOR IS ONE!
HE COMES FROM MY VILLAGE, DEEP IN THE CARPATHIAN MOUNTAINS!

"HE LIVED THERE OVER A HUNDRED YEARS AGO. THE PEOPLE OF MY VILLAGE WERE POOR, BUT ***COURAGEOUS!*** THEY REFUSED TO TOLERATE EVIL DWELLING THERE.

"THEY HUNTED THE MONSTER, KNOWING HE MUST BE DESTROYED! BUT, HE ESCAPED AND LEFT THE MOUNTAINS."

AS THE LAST DESCENDENT OF MY VILLAGE, *I* MUST FINISH WHAT THEY SET OUT TO DO!

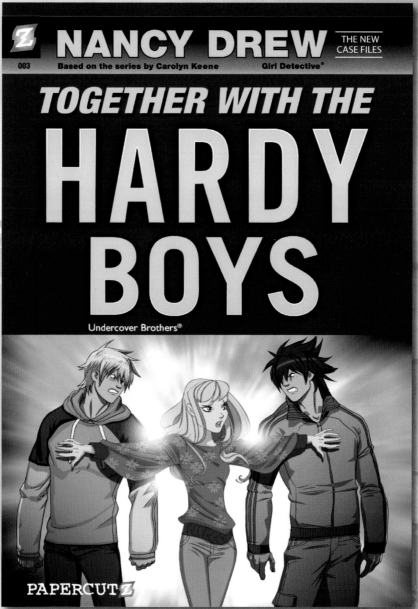